A MOLDY MYSTERY

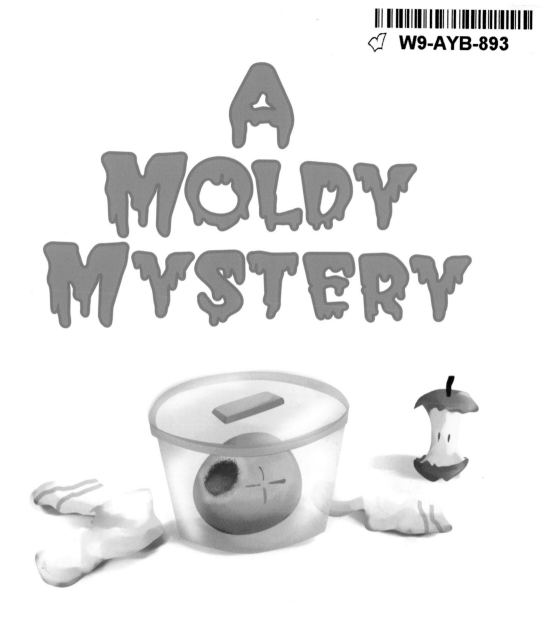

by Michelle Knudsen
illustrated by Barry Gott

The Kane Press
New York

To Juliana, the Moldinator, who left no spore unturned and faced actual real-life mold in the pursuit of science—M.K.

To Rose—B.G.

Acknowledgements: Our thanks to Denise Boltas King, Life Sciences Exhibit Developer, Exploratorium, San Francisco for helping to make this book as accurate as possible.

Text copyright © 2006 by Kane Press, Inc.
Illustrations copyright © 2006 by Barry Gott.

Library of Congress Cataloging-in-Publication Data

Knudsen, Michelle.
  A moldy mystery / by Michelle Knudsen ; illustrated by Barry Gott.
    p. cm. — (Science solves it!)
  "Mold - grades: 1-3."
  Summary: When messy Wayne goes away to camp, his younger brother Jeff throws out some old food containers that he finds in their room, but then he learns that Wayne is working on a science project about mold, and he must try to recreate the experiment before Wayne gets home.
  ISBN: 978-1-57565-167-5 (alk. paper)
  [1. Molds (Fungi)—Fiction. 2. Science—Experiments—Fiction. 3. Brothers—Fiction.] I. Gott, Barry, ill. II. Title. III. Series.
  PZ7.K7835Mol 2006
  [E]—dc22

                                     2005021199

eISBN: 978-1-57565-612-0

10 9 8 7 6 5 4

First published in the United States of America in 2006 by Kane Press, Inc.
Printed at Worzalla Publishing, Stevens Point, WI, U.S.A., May 2013.

Science Solves It! is a registered trademark of Kane Press, Inc.

Book Design: Edward Miller

Visit us online at **www.kanepress.com**

 Like us on Facebook
facebook.com/kanepress

 Follow us on Twitter
@kanepress

My brother Wayne is a total slob. I like things neat. But Wayne's mess takes over our whole room. It drives me crazy!

"How come your mom doesn't make Wayne clean up?" asks my friend Kayla.

"She thinks he's so busy studying and being smart that he doesn't have time to clean," I tell her. "As long as he keeps getting great marks, Mom doesn't seem to mind the mess."

Today Wayne is leaving for two weeks at science camp. Now's my chance to clean this place up!

"Bye, Kiddo," Wayne says, messing up my hair. I just sigh. He's always doing that.

He's gone! Finally I can get to work.

Kayla inches toward the door. "Gotta go, Jeff!" she says.

When I start cleaning, everybody gets out of my way!

I pick up Wayne's clothes and junk. It isn't easy!

I stack his magazines in a neat pile. "Hello, floor," I say. "Nice to see you again."

I find some stinky old socks by Wayne's bed.

I decide to look *under* the bed, too. That's when I find a bunch of plastic containers.

Good grief! They still have food in them. Old food covered with mold!

I toss everything in a big garbage bag and drag it out to the trash.

The next morning I hear my mom on the phone. She's talking about Wayne.

"Yes, I'm sure he'll have fun at camp," she says. "You know how he loves science. The minute school ended he started a big project—something to do with mold. He's really excited about it."

I freeze. My stomach flips and flops. Mold? A project about mold? Oh, no!

It's Alive!
It's not a plant. It's not an animal. It's MOLD! Mold, like mushrooms, is a kind of fungus—a living thing similar to both plants and animals.

I race outside. But it's too late. The garbage truck is just turning the corner.

Wayne is going to kill me!

I run back inside to call Kayla.

"Calm down, Jeff," she says. "I'll be right over."

"Wayne is going to kill you," Kayla says.

"What should I do?" I moan.

Kayla thinks for a minute. "Maybe you could try to grow some new mold."

Grow more mold! Why didn't I think of that?

Where Does Mold Come From?

Instead of seeds, mold has spores. Spores float around in the air like dandelion seeds. They can grow new mold where they land.

I find Wayne's science-club notebook.

The good news is that he's written some
notes on his project.

The bad news is that his handwriting is as
messy as he is.

"How do his teachers read this stuff?" I groan.

"I can make out a few letters," says Kayla. "Give me a sec."

She works on the notes like they're a secret code. She's good with stuff like that. "M-blank-L-D," she mumbles. "That looks like 'mold.'"

I'm so nervous, I polish my alarm clock while I wait.

Will different kinds of mold grow on different kinds of food?
- strawberries
- orange
- cup of coffee
- bread
- cupcake
- spaghetti sprinkled with sugar

"I've got it!" Kayla shouts. "He was trying to grow mold on different kinds of food."

"You're a genius!" I say. "Let's raid the kitchen."

Jackpot! The fridge is full of leftovers.

I pour one cup of coffee and sprinkle a little sugar on some pasta.

Kayla grabs an orange.

We hunt up six plastic containers, put the food inside them, and go upstairs.

Did You Know?
Mold can grow on almost anything—foods, plants, wood, wallpaper, carpeting, paint, wet paper products, dust, and even inside space stations!

"Now what do we do?" I ask Kayla. "How do we get the mold to grow?"

"I don't know," she says. "Doesn't it just grow on its own, even if you don't want it to?"

"Let's check the Internet," I say.

Did You Know?
All mold needs to grow is: oxygen, the right temperature, moisture, and something to eat.

"Saved!" shouts Kayla. "There are tons of sites on mold."

We press the print button.

SLIME MOLD

One kind of fungus—nicknamed "slime mold"—looks just like dog vomit! Slime mold has fooled plenty of gardeners into thinking their dogs were sick to their stomachs. Yuck!

Just what the doctor ordered! One kind of mold is called *Penicillium*. It is used to make penicillin, a medicine that has saved millions of lives.

Some types of mold are okay to eat. Did you ever have blue cheese? It's full of mold!

There are thousands of kinds of mold. Some kinds are powdery blue-green. Some are fluffy gray-white. Lots of molds that grow indoors are pitch black.

Green plants can make their own food. But mold can't. Mold is a decomposer—a living thing that breaks down dead things for food.

Mold breaks down rotting plant material. This material goes back into the soil so that new plants can grow. Without mold, the earth would be overrun with dead plants!

"You know, the Fun with Fungus site says that mold grows faster in dark, moist places," I tell Kayla.

"It's dark under the bed," she says. "But it's not moist."

"Good point," I tell her. We add water to the samples and shove them under the bed.

"Now we wait," Kayla says.

Helpful Hints from the Mold Police
Most kinds of mold aren't good for you. Don't eat or sniff them! (They don't smell great, anyway.)

I check the samples every morning and take
notes. But I don't see a speck of mold.

What if it doesn't grow before Wayne gets
back? I'm starting to feel really nervous.

All I can think about is mold!

That night I have a bad dream. A big, drippy
mold monster creeps out from under Wayne's
bed and tries to eat me! *Yikes!*

I wake up all sweaty. The thought of mold is making me sick. But I take a deep breath and check the containers.

Whoa!
The strawberries have white furry spots. We've got mold!

The next day I find pink slime on the pasta. There's green fuzz on the coffee the day after that.

And the orange is starting to look really disgusting!

But there's still no mold on the bread—and none on the cupcake. I panic.

MOLDY NOTES

Day		Mold looks:
Day 3:	Strawberries	white and furry
Day 4:	Pasta	pink and slimy
Day 5:	coffee	green and fuzzy
Day 6:	Orange	green and gross!
Day 7:	Cupcake	still no mold
	Bread	still no mold

"Kayla!" I shout into the phone. "Nothing's happening to the bread and the cupcake! What's wrong with the bread and the cupcake?"

"I'm on my way," she tells me.

Kayla stares at the cupcake. "Maybe it's harder to grow mold on some things," she says.

Okay, okay. I've got to think. What's different about the bread and the cupcake?

Kayla reads my mind. "Let's look at the ingredients on the wrappers."

"Preservatives!" I yell. "That's why the mold isn't growing."

"I know a bakery where we can get stuff without preservatives," Kayla says.

I jump up. "What are we waiting for?"

Preservatives added to maintain freshness

SUPER BREAD

A **preservative** is something added to a food to help keep it from spoiling— and from growing mold! You often find preservatives in packaged or canned foods that have to last a long time.

24

We buy bread. Then we ask for a cupcake.

"Don't you want two?" asks the lady behind the counter.

"Oh, we're not going to eat it," I explain. "We're going to grow mold on it."

The lady makes a face. "Sounds lovely."

Just Like
MAMA'S
All Natural!
No Preservatives!

The bakery bread works! In no time at all it grows white wisps and black dots and green bumps. A few days later I spot the first speck of mold on the cupcake.

"*Whew!* I never thought I'd be glad to see moldy food!" I tell Kayla. "And just in time. Wayne's coming home from camp tomorrow."

I wake up early the next morning. I'm a nervous wreck. When Wayne finally gets home, I don't even say hi.

"There's something I've got to tell you," I blurt out. "I accidentally threw out your mold project."

Wayne just looks at me.

I talk very fast. "Don't get mad!" I say. "Kayla and I found your notes and even though we could hardly read them we started the project over and grew some new mold for you."

"Jeff wrote everything down," Kayla adds.

"Take a look under your bed," I tell Wayne.

"Wow!" Wayne looks impressed. "This is some nice-looking mold," he says. "But my science-club project is over at Diane's house. You must have found some old lunch containers I forgot to throw out."

He messes up my hair and goes downstairs.

Kayla and I stare at each other.

"I can't believe it!" I groan. "We did all that for nothing!"

"Well, at least we learned a lot about mold," Kayla says.

"I learned some other things, too," I tell her.

"Like what?"

"First, never pick up Wayne's mess," I say. "It spreads faster than mold! Second, never *ever* clean under Wayne's bed. Who knows WHAT you might find there?"

Helpful Hints from the Mold Busters
To keep mold where it belongs (outside!):
• control moisture in your home • clean out your fridge • repair any water leaks • don't leave old lunch containers under your bed!

We can conduct a simple experiment!

Grr!

THINK LIKE A SCIENTIST

Jeff and Kayla think like scientists—and so can you!
Scientists try out their ideas by doing experiments. Jeff and Kayla use Wayne's notes to conduct a simple experiment: a real-life mold-growing operation. Just like scientists, they keep checking their mold samples and testing out new ideas until they get the experiment right!

Look Back

- Look at pages 13–14. What is Wayne's science project? How do Jeff and Kayla prepare for the experiment?
- What things does Jeff discover on pages 18 and 24? How does he change the experiment based on what he has learned? Do the new ideas work? Why do you think so?

Try This!

Make your very own Mold Terrarium!
Step 1: You'll need a clear, lidded container. (Make sure you're allowed to throw it away after the experiment.)
Step 2: For a rainbow of results, try inserting a few different foods—fruits, veggies, bread, and cheese. (Do not use meat or fish. Moldy food smells bad. Rotting meat smells worse.)
Step 3: Check your terrarium in a couple days. Be amazed! Or grossed out. Trash the rotten food after two weeks.
Brainy Bonus: Try keeping Mold Terrariums in the sunlight and in the dark, or in warm and cool temperatures. How does the mold grow differently in different places?